HISTORY SPEAKS

PICTURE BOOKS PLUS READER'S THEATER

Annie Shapiro and the

CLOTHING WORKERS' STRIKE

BY **MARLENE TARG BRILL**

ILLUSTRATED BY **JAMEL AKIB**

MILLBROOK PRESS / MINNEAPOLIS

A special thanks to Annie's family, Dena, Harry, and Miffie, who continue her tradition of fighting for what's right —M.T.B.

Text copyright © 2011 by Marlene Targ Brill
Illustrations © 2011 by Lerner Publishing Group, Inc.

Millbrook Press
A division of Lerner Publishing Group, Inc.
241 First Avenue North
Minneapolis, MN 55401 U.S.A.

Website address: www.lernerbooks.com

The author wishes to thank the many individuals from Spertus College, the Chicago Historical Museum, the University of Illinois Special Collections, the Chicago Jewish Historical Society, the Illinois State Library, the Illinois State Archives, Hull House, the Illinois Labor History Society, and Roosevelt University who shared their information.

The images in this book are used with the permission of: Dena Targ, p. 32; DN-0056264, Chicago Daily News negatives collection, Chicago Historical Society, p. 33.

Library of Congress Cataloging-in-Publication Data

Brill, Marlene Targ.
  Annie Shapiro and the clothing workers' strike / by Marlene Targ Brill ; illustrated by Jamel Akib.
    p.   cm. — (History speaks)
  Includes bibliographical references.
  ISBN: 978–1–58013–672–3 (lib. bdg. : alk. paper)
  1. Shapiro Glick, Annie. 2. Garment Workers' Strike, Chicago, 1910–1911. 3. Strikes and lockouts—Clothing trade—Illinois—Chicago—History—20th century—Juvenile literature. 4. Women clothing workers—Illinois—Chicago—History—20th century—Juvenile literature. 5. Women in the labor movement—Illinois—Chicago—History—20th century—Juvenile literature. I. Title.
  HD5325.C621910 B75 2011
  331.892'887097731109041—dc22   2009051812

Manufactured in the United States of America
1 – BP – 7/15/10

CONTENTS

CHICAGO

September 22, 1910

Annie awoke before the sun rose. She tossed coal into the stove, dressed, and boiled oats for breakfast. She helped her four younger brothers and sisters get ready for school while her mother fed the two babies.

Once everyone finished breakfast, Annie kissed her parents and grabbed her lunch. After her mother became sick five years ago, Annie had to quit school and start working. The money she earned at the clothing factory helped to pay the doctor bills. Now Annie was seventeen and still working.

Annie ran fourteen blocks over dusty wooden sidewalks. She never wanted to be late to work. Every late minute meant the foreman paid her less for that day.

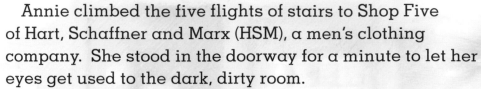

Annie climbed the five flights of stairs to Shop Five
of Hart, Schaffner and Marx (HSM), a men's clothing
company. She stood in the doorway for a minute to let her
eyes get used to the dark, dirty room.

"In ten hours, I'll see sunlight again," Annie told herself.

The other workers greeted her with smiles. They looked
up to Annie. When the foreman in charge of the shop
was mean or treated someone unfairly, Annie spoke out.
She had arrived from Russia a little more than five years
earlier, but she spoke English better than the others. They
counted on her to be their voice.

Annie sat behind a pile of cloth pieces. She picked up her needle and quickly began sewing pockets for men's pants. Sewing one pocket was easy. But sewing pockets all day hurt her fingers and made her eyes tired and back sore.

Making one pair of pants took fifty different steps. Workers at each HSM shop sewed only one or two steps. Other workers at a main factory downtown sewed all the parts together to finish the pants.

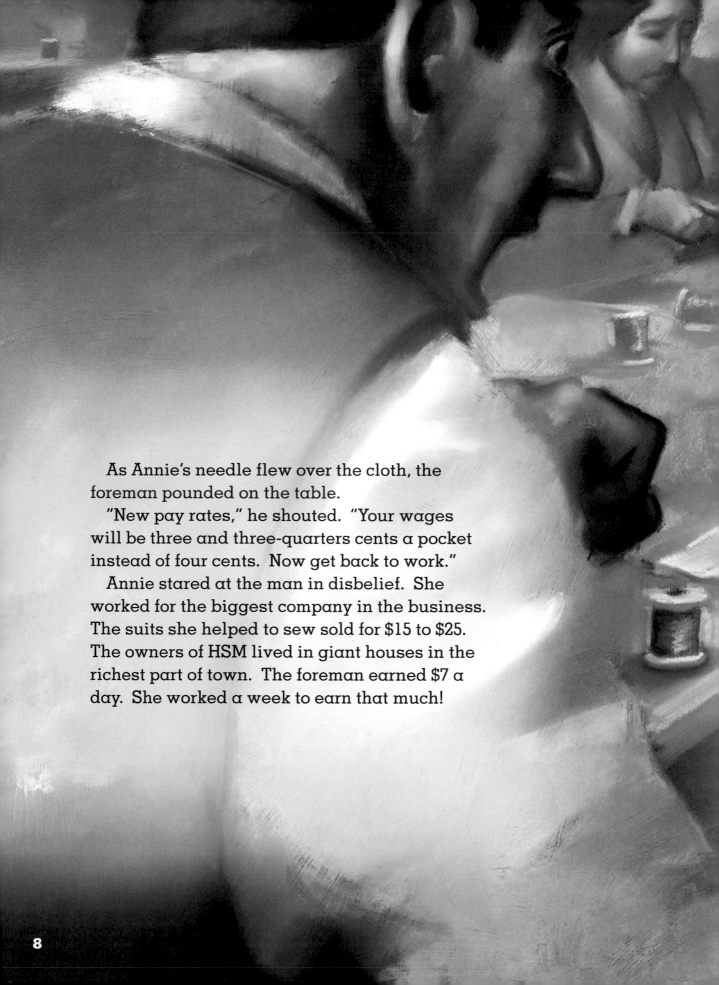

As Annie's needle flew over the cloth, the foreman pounded on the table.

"New pay rates," he shouted. "Your wages will be three and three-quarters cents a pocket instead of four cents. Now get back to work."

Annie stared at the man in disbelief. She worked for the biggest company in the business. The suits she helped to sew sold for $15 to $25. The owners of HSM lived in giant houses in the richest part of town. The foreman earned $7 a day. She worked a week to earn that much!

Annie's cheeks flushed with anger.

"Why can he do as he pleases? Why do company owners let foremen make the shop rules?" she thought, making a fist.

Last month, Annie's foreman had added a different rule.

"You all will need to sew more pockets for your day's pay." he had said. "Work faster."

Annie often had to stay late to finish. And now he was cutting their pay just to keep more for himself. Annie could not take it anymore.

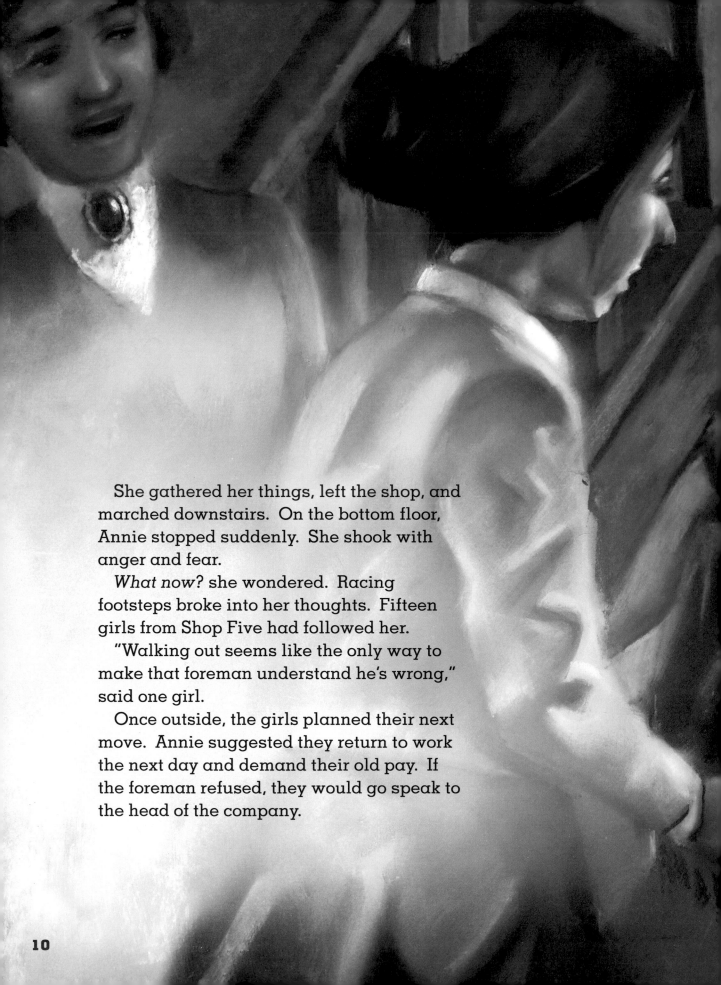

She gathered her things, left the shop, and marched downstairs. On the bottom floor, Annie stopped suddenly. She shook with anger and fear.

What now? she wondered. Racing footsteps broke into her thoughts. Fifteen girls from Shop Five had followed her.

"Walking out seems like the only way to make that foreman understand he's wrong," said one girl.

Once outside, the girls planned their next move. Annie suggested they return to work the next day and demand their old pay. If the foreman refused, they would go speak to the head of the company.

Annie ran home to tell her mother and father what
had happened.

"We all went out," Annie told her parents. "We just had
to be seen as people."

The room turned quiet. The silence worried Annie. She
fiddled with her buttons. Her father was a gentle man.
But the family needed her pay. She could lose her job for
walking out. Would he be angry?

"You have a good heart," her mother said after a while.
"But who will marry such a strong-willed girl?"

Annie bit her lip and turned to her father. He held out
his arms to her and smiled.

"I'm proud of you," he said. "You must do what is right."

Annie buried herself in his hug. She felt tired from
worry. But she was excited by what her father had said.
She knew she must fight for what was fair—both for
herself and for the others.

Annie and her friends returned to Shop Five the next day.

"Return our old pay," they told the foreman. "And treat us with respect!"

The foreman refused to change his mind. "There are plenty of workers to take your place," he growled.

Annie led the girls from floor to floor to other HSM shops. "Speak out," Annie said. "Demand your rights!"

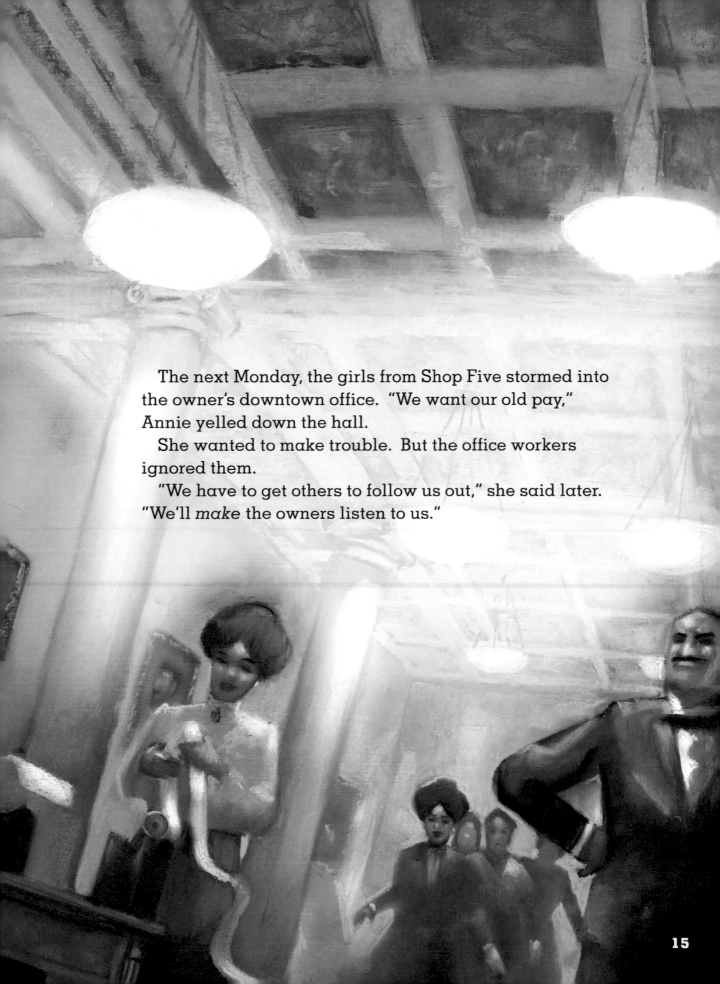

The next Monday, the girls from Shop Five stormed into the owner's downtown office. "We want our old pay," Annie yelled down the hall.

She wanted to make trouble. But the office workers ignored them.

"We have to get others to follow us out," she said later. "We'll *make* the owners listen to us."

That evening, about one hundred workers met at Hull House, the neighborhood center. Annie often went to Hull House with other workers for evening classes and dances. She knew she would find support there.

The HSM girls shared stories of how badly they were treated. They asked everyone to stop working and walk out. They would all go on strike. The strike would force owners of clothing companies to treat them better and pay them more.

The following day, the girls went to the United Garment Workers Union (UGW). The UGW helped garment workers get and keep their rights. Even though HSM didn't let employees join unions, Annie hoped the UGW would help them. But the men who led the UGW just laughed at the girls.

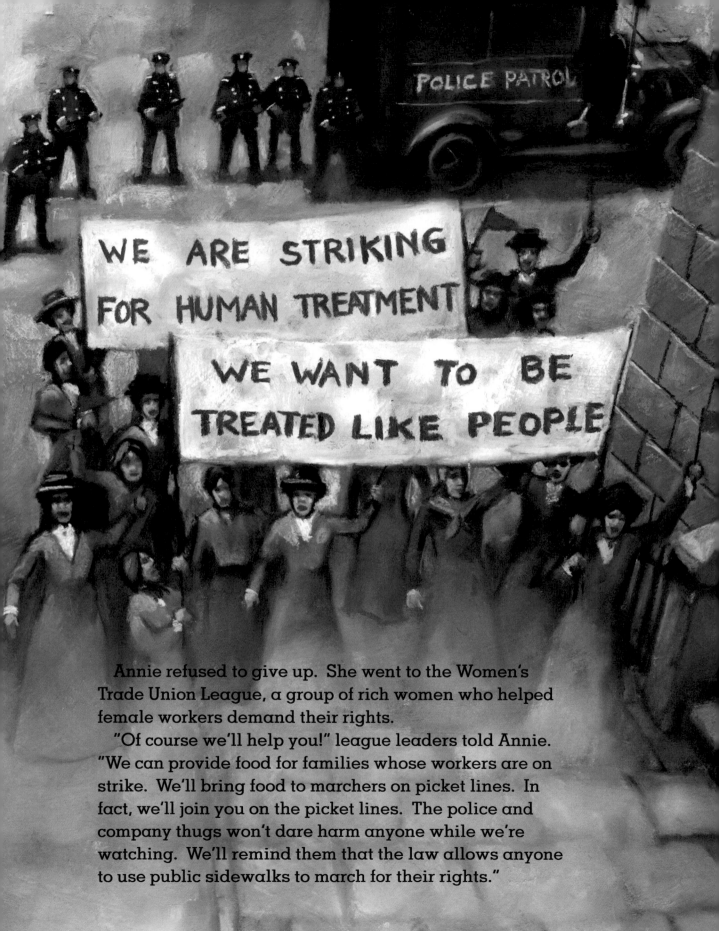

WE ARE STRIKING
FOR HUMAN TREATMENT

WE WANT TO BE
TREATED LIKE PEOPLE

POLICE PATROL

Annie refused to give up. She went to the Women's Trade Union League, a group of rich women who helped female workers demand their rights.

"Of course we'll help you!" league leaders told Annie. "We can provide food for families whose workers are on strike. We'll bring food to marchers on picket lines. In fact, we'll join you on the picket lines. The police and company thugs won't dare harm anyone while we're watching. We'll remind them that the law allows anyone to use public sidewalks to march for their rights."

Each day, Annie and others paraded back and forth in front of HSM shops. As Annie neared each shop, she blew a whistle. The sound signaled workers inside to walk out.

"We're coming," one worker yelled through the open window. "Keep the foreman from locking the doors!"

By the end of the week, two thousand workers had left their jobs to join the strike.

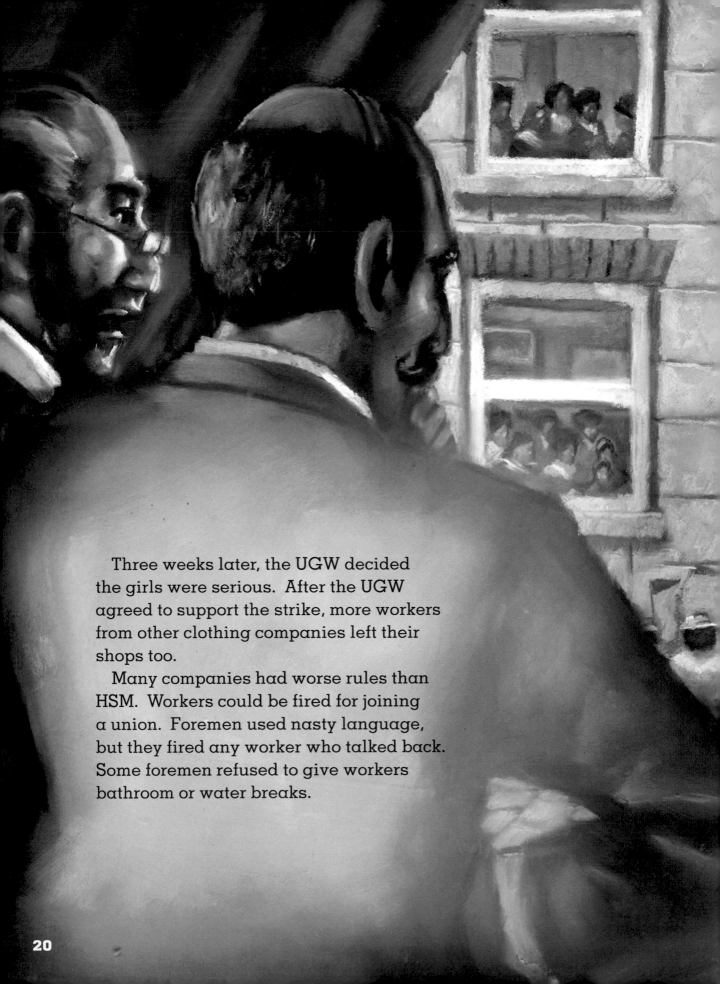

Three weeks later, the UGW decided
the girls were serious. After the UGW
agreed to support the strike, more workers
from other clothing companies left their
shops too.

Many companies had worse rules than
HSM. Workers could be fired for joining
a union. Foremen used nasty language,
but they fired any worker who talked back.
Some foremen refused to give workers
bathroom or water breaks.

Bosses often did not know how the foremen treated the workers. Annie's bosses were surprised by the strike. "Our workers are happy," they said. "This strike is just a few troublemakers stirring everyone up."

But the strike spread. Within a month, forty thousand workers were on strike all over the city. Annie could not believe what she had started.

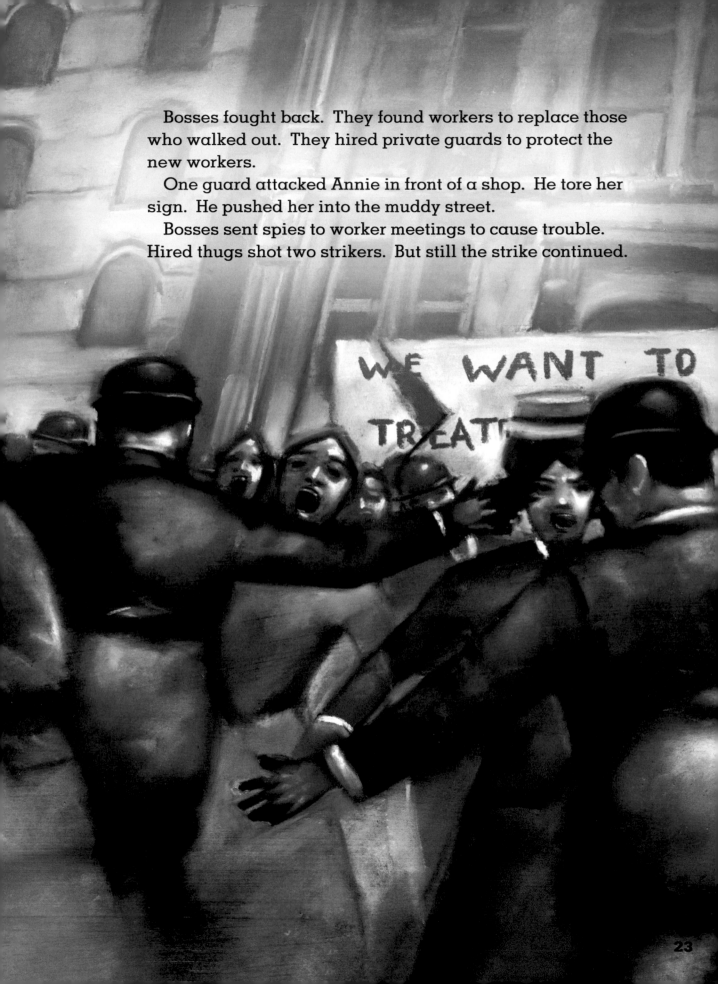

Bosses fought back. They found workers to replace those who walked out. They hired private guards to protect the new workers.

One guard attacked Annie in front of a shop. He tore her sign. He pushed her into the muddy street.

Bosses sent spies to worker meetings to cause trouble. Hired thugs shot two strikers. But still the strike continued.

Food ran out for some striking families. Many could not
pay their rent. The Women's League wanted to raise more
money to help the workers. But the league needed help. Their
president thought the group could raise more money if some
of the workers would share their stories. She asked Annie to
talk to league members about working in a shop.

Annie had never made a speech before. Until this day,
she had been fearless. She had argued with union leaders
and company owners. She had faced police with clubs and
paddy wagons. But her hands turned sweaty at the thought of
speaking in front of rich women.

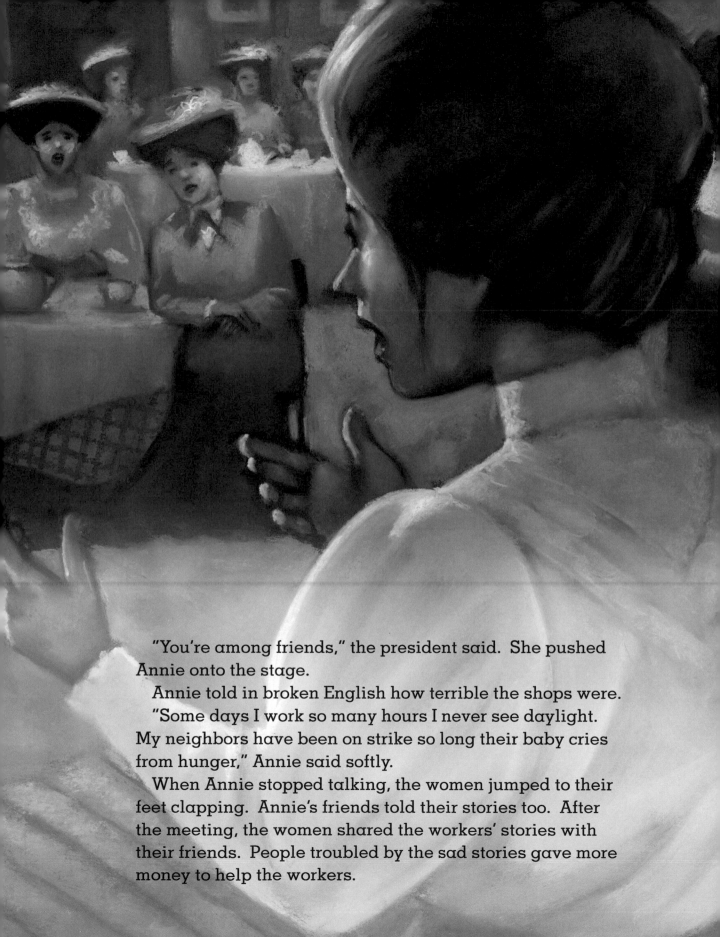

"You're among friends," the president said. She pushed Annie onto the stage.

Annie told in broken English how terrible the shops were.

"Some days I work so many hours I never see daylight. My neighbors have been on strike so long their baby cries from hunger," Annie said softly.

When Annie stopped talking, the women jumped to their feet clapping. Annie's friends told their stories too. After the meeting, the women shared the workers' stories with their friends. People troubled by the sad stories gave more money to help the workers.

Many months after the strike had begun, Mr. Schaffner from HSM finally offered his workers a deal. He still wouldn't allow a union. But he agreed to create a team of HSM workers from the shops and the downtown office to listen to workers' problems and find ways to solve them.

This was a huge step. Now the workers would have a say in running the shops. Foremen would have to listen to their workers.

Before the strike could end, workers all over the city had to vote on the plan. At Hull House, Annie helped pass out copies of the plan printed in eight different languages. She was proud to vote in English.

Afterward, Annie helped count votes. Counting lasted many days. But in the end, the plan to end the strike passed. Three days later, Annie and two thousand other workers returned to work at the HSM shops.

"Things are better now that we can speak out against unfair rules without fear of being fired," Annie told her parents. Her father hugged her. "Work is still hard. But I'm glad my walking out made a difference."

Author's Note

Annie's real name was Hannah Shapiro, but her HMS friends nicknamed her Annie. In 1905, Annie came with her family from a Russian village to Chicago, Illinois. In Russia, her father had been a rabbi, a Jewish leader and teacher. In the United States, he taught Jewish studies. The Shapiros rented a small apartment with a bathroom on Chicago's West Side.

At first, Annie went to school nearby. She was already twelve, and she felt silly in class with first graders. Still, she stayed to learn English. But after five months, her mother got sick. Annie went to work to help her family pay doctor bills.

The city had laws against hiring such young workers. But greedy bosses broke the law. They could pay children like Annie less than adults. Sometimes city workers overlooked places where children worked. Other times, bosses hid working children when city inspectors visited.

Most men's clothing in the United States was made in Chicago. Annie sewed for two different companies. After five years, she found work at HSM. Each day, Annie and other workers bent over tables in a gloomy room. They sewed for ten hours while a foreman barked orders.

After the strike, the new HSM team of workers and bosses agreed to raise workers' pay. The strike improved conditions at Annie's shop. Other clothing companies, however, refused

THE SHAPIRO FAMILY.
ANNIE IS IN THE BACK ROW ON THE RIGHT.

STRIKING WORKERS IN CHICAGO IN 1910

to give workers their rights for another seven years. But the strike alerted Illinois lawmakers to problems with worker rights. They asked Annie and other strikers to tell them why workers had walked out. They wanted to help the workers.

After the strike, Annie worked for three more years. In 1914, she married Julius Glick, a printer. She stopped working to raise two children. Annie rarely talked about her role in the great strike. But her brave stand had brought workers together to fight for their rights. This movement led to a giant national union, Workers United.

As an author, writing Annie's story was a special treat. Annie was the aunt of my brother's wife, Dena Epstein Targ. Now Annie feels like family to me too. Dena, her brother Harry Epstein, and their cousin Miffie Nagorsky, helped me learn about Annie and their family. I visited places where Annie lived, worked, and marched for her rights. I read newspaper and magazine articles and private papers about the strike and the times. These original documents and interviews helped me tell Annie's true story.

Performing Reader's Theater

Dear Student,

Reader's Theater is a dramatic reading. It is a little like a play, but you don't need to memorize your lines. Here are some tips that will help you do your best in a Reader's Theater performance.

BEFORE THE PERFORMANCE

- **Choose your part:** Your teacher may assign parts, or you may be allowed to choose your own part. The character you play does not need to be the same age as you. A boy can play the part of a girl, and a girl can play the part of a boy. That's why it's called acting!

- **Find your lines:** Your character's name is always the same color. The name at the bottom of each page tells you which character has the first line on the next page. If you are allowed to write on your script, highlight your lines. If you cannot write on the script, you may want to use sticky flags to mark your lines.

- **Check pronunciations of words:** If your character's lines include any words you aren't sure how to pronounce, check the pronunciation guide on page 45. If a word isn't there or you still aren't sure how to say it, check a dictionary or ask a teacher, librarian, or other adult.

- **Use your emotions:** Think about how your character feels in the story. If you imagine how your character feels, the audience will hear the emotion in your voice.

- **Use your imagination:** Think about how your character's voice might sound. For example, an old man's voice will sound different from a baby's voice. If you do change your voice, make sure the audience can still understand the words you are saying.

- **Practice your lines:** Even though you do not need to memorize your lines, you should still be comfortable reading them. Read your lines aloud often so they flow smoothly.

DURING THE PERFORMANCE

- **Keep your script away from your face but high enough to read:** If you cover your face with your script, you block your voice from the audience. If you have your script too low, you need to tip your head down farther to read it and the audience won't be able to hear you.

- **Use eye contact:** Good Reader's Theater performers look at the audience as much as they look at their scripts. If you look down, the sound of your voice goes down to the script and not out to the audience.

- **Speak clearly:** Make sure you are loud enough. Say all your words carefully. Be sure not to read too quickly. Remember, if you feel nervous, you may start to speak faster than usual.

- **Use facial expressions and gestures:** Your facial expressions and gestures (hand movements) help the audience know how your character is feeling. If your character is happy, smile. If your character is angry, cross your arms and be sure not to smile.

- **Have fun:** It's okay if you feel nervous. If you make a mistake, just try to relax and keep going. Reader's Theater is meant to be fun for the actors and the audience!

Cast of Characters

ANNIE SHAPIRO:
a seventeen-year old girl who
works in a clothing factory

READER 1:
a foreman at the clothing factory,
Annie's father, a male worker

READER 2:
a female worker, Annie's mother,
the league president

NARRATOR 1

NARRATOR 2

ALL:
everyone except sound

SOUND:
This part has no lines. The person in this role
is in charge of the sound effects.
Find the sound effects for this script
at www.historyspeaksbooks.com.

NARRATOR 1: In 1910, Annie Shapiro was seventeen years old. She lived in Chicago, Illinois. She had been working since she was twelve years old to help her family.

NARRATOR 2: Annie woke early to make breakfast and help her younger brothers and sisters get ready for school. Once everyone finished breakfast, Annie kissed her parents and grabbed her lunch. She ran fourteen blocks over dusty wooden sidewalks to get to her job.

SOUND: [running feet]

ANNIE: I can't be late to work! Every late minute means the foreman pays me less for the day.

NARRATOR 1: Annie climbed five flights of stairs to Shop Five of HSM, a men's clothing company. The room where she worked was dark and dirty.

ANNIE: In ten hours, I'll be done with work and I'll see sunlight again.

NARRATOR 2: The other workers greeted Annie with smiles. They looked up to Annie. When the foreman in charge of the shop was mean or treated someone unfairly, Annie spoke out. The others counted on her to be their voice.

NARRATOR 1: Annie sat behind a pile of cloth pieces. She picked up her needle and quickly began sewing pockets for men's pants.

Next Page — **ANNIE**

ANNIE: Sewing one pocket is easy. But sewing pockets all day hurts my fingers and makes my eyes tired and my back sore.

NARRATOR 2: As Annie's needle flew over the cloth, the foreman pounded on the table.

SOUND: [pounding]

READER 1 (AS FOREMAN): Listen up! New pay rates. You will not be paid four cents a pocket anymore. Instead, you will get three and three-quarters cents a pocket. Get back to work.

NARRATOR 1: Annie stared at the man in disbelief. She worked for the biggest company in the business. The foreman earned seven dollars a day. She worked a week to earn that much!

ANNIE: Why can he do as he pleases? Why do company owners let foremen make the shop rules?

NARRATOR 2: Last month, Annie's foreman had added a different rule.

READER 1 (AS FOREMAN): You all will need to sew more pockets for your day's pay. Work faster.

NARRATOR 1: Annie often had to stay late to finish. And now the foreman was cutting their pay just to keep more for himself. Annie could not take it anymore. She gathered her things, left the shop, and marched downstairs. On the bottom floor, Annie stopped suddenly.

Next Page — **ANNIE**

ANNIE: What now?

NARRATOR 2: Fifteen girls from Shop Five had followed her.

READER 2 (AS FEMALE WORKER): Walking out seems like the only way to make the foreman understand he's wrong.

ANNIE: We should return to work tomorrow and demand our old pay. If the foreman refuses, we'll go speak to the head of the company.

NARRATOR 1: Annie ran home to tell her mother and father what had happened.

ANNIE: We all went out. We just had to be seen as people.

NARRATOR 2: The room turned quiet. Annie's family needed her pay, but she could lose her job for walking out. Would her parents be angry?

READER 2 (AS ANNIE'S MOTHER): You have a good heart. But who will marry such a strong-willed girl?

ANNIE: Father, what do you think?

READER 1 (AS ANNIE'S FATHER): I'm proud of you. You must do what is right.

NARRATOR 1: Annie and her friends returned to Shop Five the next day.

ANNIE AND READER 2 (AS FEMALE WORKER): Return our old pay. And treat us with respect!

Next Page — **READER 1**

READER 1 (AS FOREMAN): I don't need you. There are plenty of workers to take your place.

NARRATOR 2: Annie led the girls to other HSM shops.

ANNIE: Speak out. Demand your rights!

NARRATOR 1: The next Monday, the girls from Shop Five stormed into the owner's downtown office.

ANNIE: We want our old pay!

NARRATOR 2: Annie wanted to make trouble. But the office workers ignored her and the other girls.

ANNIE: We have to get others to follow us out. We'll make the owners listen to us.

NARRATOR 1: That evening, about one hundred workers met at Hull House, the neighborhood center. The workers shared stories of how badly they were treated. They asked everyone to stop working and walk out. They would all go on strike. The strike would force owners of clothing companies to treat them better and pay them more.

NARRATOR 2: The next day, the girls went to the United Garment Workers Union, known as the UGW. The UGW helped garment workers get and keep their rights. Even though HSM didn't allow unions, Annie hoped the UGW would help them. But the men who led the UGW just laughed.

SOUND: [laughter]

Next Page — **ANNIE**

ANNIE: I won't give up. Let's go to the Women's Trade Union League. They help female workers demand their rights.

READER 2 (AS LEAGUE PRESIDENT): Oh, Annie, of course we'll help you! We can provide food for families whose workers are on strike. We'll bring food to marchers on picket lines. In fact, we'll join you on the picket lines. The police and company thugs won't dare harm anyone while we're watching. We'll remind them that the law allows anyone to use public sidewalks to march for their rights.

NARRATOR 1: Each day, Annie and others walked back and forth in front of HSM shops. As Annie neared each shop, she blew a whistle. The sound signaled workers inside to walk out.

SOUND: [whistle]

READER 1 (AS MALE WORKER): Annie! We're coming. Don't let the foreman lock the doors!

NARRATOR 2: By the end of the week, two thousand workers had left their jobs to join the strike. Three weeks later, the UGW decided to help. More workers from other clothing companies left their shops too.

NARRATOR 1: Many companies had worse rules than HSM. Workers could be fired for joining a union. Many foremen used nasty language, and they fired any worker who talked back. Some foremen wouldn't even give workers bathroom or water breaks.

Next Page — **NARRATOR 2**

NARRATOR 2: Bosses often did not know how the foremen treated the workers. Annie's bosses were surprised by the strike.

READER 1 (AS BOSS): Our workers are happy. This strike is just a few people making trouble. They're upsetting the other workers.

ANNIE: I can hardly believe how big the strike has become! More than forty thousand workers are on strike all over the city.

NARRATOR 1: Bosses fought back. They found workers to replace those who walked out. They hired private guards to protect the new workers. One guard attacked Annie in front of a shop. He tore her sign and pushed her into the muddy street.

NARRATOR 2: Food ran out for some striking families. Many could not pay their rent. The Women's League wanted to raise more money to help the workers.

READER 2 (AS LEAGUE PRESIDENT): Annie, we could raise more money if some of the workers will share their stories. Can you talk to the league members about working in a shop?

ANNIE: I've never made a speech before. Even though I have argued with company bosses and faced the police, I feel nervous. My hands are sweating.

READER 2 (AS LEAGUE PRESIDENT): You're among friends. You can do it.

Next Page — **NARRATOR 1**

NARRATOR 1: Annie took a deep breath and began to speak.

ANNIE: Some days, I work so many hours I never see daylight. My neighbors have been on strike so long their baby cries from hunger.

NARRATOR 1: After Annie was finished, the women jumped to their feet clapping.

SOUND: [clapping]

NARRATOR 2: Annie's friends told their stories too. People gave more money to help the workers.

NARRATOR 1: Many months after the strike had begun, HSM finally offered the workers a deal.

READER 1 (AS BOSS): We will create a team of workers. Some workers will be from the shops. Others will be from the downtown office. This team will listen to workers' problems. Then it will find ways to solve them.

NARRATOR 1: Now the workers would have a say in running the shops. The foremen would have to listen to their workers.

NARRATOR 2: Before the strike could end, workers all over the city needed to vote on the plan. Annie helped pass out copies of the plan printed in eight different languages.

Next Page — **NARRATOR 1**

NARRATOR 1: Afterward, Annie helped count votes. Counting lasted many days. But in the end, the plan to end the strike passed. Annie and two thousand other workers returned to work at the HSM shops.

READER 1 (AS ANNIE'S FATHER) AND **READER 2 (AS ANNIE'S MOTHER):** Annie, we're so proud of you.

ANNIE: Things are better now that we can speak out against unfair rules without fear of being fired. Work is still hard. But I'm glad my walking out made a difference.

ALL: The end.

Pronunciation Guide

foreman: FOR-man
league: LEEG
Marx: MARKS
Schaffner: SHAF-nur
Shapiro: shah-PEER-oh
union: YOON-yuhn

Glossary

foreman: the person in charge of a group of workers
garment: a piece of clothing
Hull House: a community organization that offered programs and services to poor families who moved to Chicago from other countries
paddy wagon: a police vehicle used to carry prisoners
picket: when someone walks or stands in front of a workplace to protest what happens inside
strike: when workers walk out to make demands of their boss or protest work conditions
thugs: violent people
union: a group of workers who join together to improve wages and working conditions
United Garment Workers Union: the first national group to speak for workers who made men's clothing
Women's Trade Union League: a group of women who worked at Hull House to help poor women improve their lives

Selected Bibliography

Buhle, Mari Jo. "Socialist Women and the 'Girl Strikers,' Chicago, 1910." *Signs* 1, no. 4 (Summer 1976): 1,039–1,051.

"Chicago at the Front: A Condensed History of the Garment Workers' Strike." *Life and Labor* 1, no. 1 (1911): 4–15.

"The Girls' Own Stories." *Life and Labor* 1, no. 2 (1911): 51–52.

Jensen, Joan. *A Needle, a Bobbin, a Strike*. Philadelphia: Temple University Press, 1984.

Sive-Tomashefsky, Rebecca. "Identifying a Lost Leader: Hannah Shapiro and the 1910 Chicago Garment Worker's Strike." *Signs* 3, no. 4 (Summer 1978): 936–939.

Weiler, Sue. "Walkout: The Chicago Men's Garment Workers Strike, 1910–1911." *Chicago History* 8, no. 4, (Winter 1979–1980): 238–249.

Women's Trade Union League of Chicago, Strike Committee. "Official Report of the Strike Committee: Chicago Garment Workers' Strike, October 29, 1910–February 18, 1911."

Further Reading and Websites

BOOKS

Bartoletti, Susan Campbell. *Kids on Strike*. New York: Sandpiper, 2003.
The author tells the story of children who played important roles in early 1900s labor strikes.

Bierman, Carol. *Journey to Ellis Island: How My Father Came to America*. Toronto: Madison Press, 2009.
This real-life Jewish family's escape from Russia to the United States mirrors Annie's move to Chicago.

Brown, Don. *Kid Blink Beats the World*. New York: Roaring Brook Press, 2004.
This picture book follows the brave newsboys who battled powerful newspaper owners in New York at the end of the 1800s to get a fair wage.

Freedman, Russell. *Immigrant Kids*. New York: Puffin, 1995.
The author presents many photos and stories of people whose families moved to U.S. cities in the early 1900s.

Freedman, Russell. *Kids at Work: Lewis Hine and the Crusade against Child Labor*. New York: Scholastic, 1994.
This book about children at work shows their struggles through photos taken by Lewis Hine in the early 1900s.

Hurd, Owen. *Chicago History for Kids: Triumphs and Tragedies of the Windy City*. Chicago: Chicago Review Press, 2007.
This book incorporates timelines, stories, photos, maps, and activities about Chicago and its history.

WEBSITES

Chicago History for Kids
http://www.chicagohistory.org/mychicago
The site offers games, puzzles, and fun facts about Chicago's history.

Immigration: Stories of Yesterday and Today
http://teacher.scholastic.com/activities/immigration/index.htm
This story of immigration throughout U.S. history includes a virtual tour of Ellis Island with early 1900s film clips by Thomas Edison.

Where Did Kids Play around Hull House?
http://tigger.uic.edu/htbin/cgiwrap/bin/urbanexp/main.cgi?&file=img/show_gallery.ptt&gallery=2
Photos and captions illustrate where the kids who lived in Hull House and the surrounding neighborhood played.

Dear Teachers and Librarians,

Congratulations on bringing Reader's Theater to your students! Reader's Theater is an excellent way for your students to develop their reading fluency. Phrasing and inflection, two important reading skills, are at the heart of Reader's Theater. Students also develop public speaking skills such as volume, pacing, and facial expression.

The traditional format of Reader's Theater is very simple. There really is no right or wrong way to do it. By following these few tips, you and your students will be ready to explore the world of Reader's Theater.

EQUIPMENT

Location: A theater or gymnasium is a fine place for a Reader's Theater performance, but staging the performance in the classroom works well too.

Scripts: Each reader will need a copy of the script. Scripts that are individually printed should be bound into binders that allow the readers to turn the pages easily. Printable scripts for all the books in this series are available at www.historyspeaksbooks.com.

Music Stands: Music stands are very helpful for the readers to set their scripts on.

Costumes: Traditional Reader's Theater does not use costumes. Dressing uniformly, such as all wearing the same color shirt, will give a group a polished look. Specific costume pieces can be used when a reader is performing multiple roles. They help the audience follow the story.

Props: Props are optional. If necessary, readers may mime or gesture to convey objects that are important to the story. Props can be used much like a costume piece to identify different characters performed by one reader. Prop suggestions for each story are available at www.historyspeaksbooks.com.

Background and Sound Effects: These aren't essential, but they can add to the fun of Reader's Theater. Customized backgrounds for each story in this series and sound effects corresponding to the scripts are available at www.historyspeaksbooks.com. You will need a screen or electronic whiteboard for the background. You will need a computer with speakers to play the sound effects.

PERFORMANCE

Staging: Readers usually face the audience in a straight line or a semicircle. If the readers are using music stands, the stands should be raised chest high. A stand should not block a reader's mouth or face, but it should allow for the reader to read without looking down too much. The main character is usually placed in the center. The narrator is on the end. In the case of multiple narrators, place one narrator on each end.

Reading: Reader's Theater scripts do not need to be memorized. However, the readers should be familiar enough with the script to maintain a fair amount of eye contact with the audience. Encourage readers to act with their voices by reading with inflection and emotion.

Blocking (stage movement): For traditional Reader's Theater, there are no blocking cues to follow. You may want to have the students turn the pages simultaneously. Some groups prefer that readers sit or turn their backs to the audience when their characters are "offstage" or have left a scene. Some groups will have their readers move about the stage, script in hand, to interact with the other readers. The choice is up to you.

Overture and Curtain Call: Before the performance, a member of the group should announce the title and the author of the piece. At the end of the performance, all readers step in front of their music stands, stand in a line, grasp hands, and bow in unison.

Please visit www.historyspeaksbooks.com for printable scripts, prop suggestions, sound effects, a background image that can be projected on a screen or electronic whiteboard, a Reader's Theater teacher's guide, and reading-level information for all roles.